DOUGAL
and the blue cat

The story of the film
retold by Jane Carruth
Pictures by Hutchings

HAMLYN
London · New York · Sydney · Toronto

Dougal – that famous star of the Magic Roundabout – was lying in bed dreaming about Florence when he heard his name being called. 'It's that cuckoo creature at it again,' he told himself. 'Why doesn't he shut up and get back into his house?'

Ever since Florence had given him the new cuckoo clock his life had been made miserable. And now Dougal pulled the sheet right up to his nose, hoping the cuckoo would take the hint. Instead, it began screeching all over again. 'Dougal! Dougal! Wakey, wakey! Get up, you lazy bones!'

'I'll teach you to call me lazy bones,' Dougal suddenly shouted, springing out of bed. 'And if you don't shut up, I'll – I'll nail up your doors and that'll be the end of you, you horrid bird!'

Satisfied that he wouldn't be hearing any more from the cuckoo, Dougal stretched and yawned. Then, out of habit, he kissed Florence's picture which he kept over his bed. But he did this without his usual

enthusiasm for, truth to tell, Dougal had something on his mind.

'It was very funny last night,' he told himself, as he made a pot of tea and sat down to drink it. 'Very funny indeed and the best thing I can do is tell somebody about it all . . .'

As he crunched his third sugar lump, Dougal considered who, among his friends of the Magic Roundabout, would be the best to tell of last night's strange happenings.

Mr. Rusty and Mr. MacHenry would certainly give him some advice, but they were usually so busy.

Brian – well, Dougal knew he had more brains than that Snail any day – so why ask him? As for Dylan, he'd most likely be still asleep. He couldn't tell Florence for it might worry her too much; and Rosalie and the boys were far too young. That left Zebedee. And the minute Dougal thought of Zebedee, he knew he was the right one to go to with a problem.

'I'll set out right away,' he decided.

As Dougal set out to walk through the Magic Garden, he met the train and, thinking there was little point in walking when he could ride, he jumped aboard.

'Just drop me off at Zebedee's place,' he called out, 'and don't take all day about it. I'm in a hurry.'

But the train was not going to hurry and Dougal began to regret ever boarding her. Slowly, slowly the train chugged her way through the Magic Garden – giving Dougal plenty of time to talk to old friends.

Presently, sly Brian Snail came skidding along and to Dougal's disgust offered to take on the train in a race.

'Go away, Brian,' said Dougal. 'Don't hold things up . . .' He spoke too soon for suddenly the train came to an abrupt stop.

'You're blocking the line!' Dougal shouted furiously, when he saw Ermintrude standing there. 'Get off the line, Ermintrude.'

But the little pink cow was enjoying herself.

'Sorry, darling,' she said. 'I just happen to love watching trains – all cows do, you know. It's in their nature.'

'I'm in a hurry,' Dougal growled. 'Please be sensible, Ermintrude. I've got to see Zebedee about something important . . .'

'Oh, very well, Dougal darling,' said Ermintrude. 'Anything to oblige you.' And away she trotted.

'I think I'll walk the rest,' said Dougal. And he jumped down from the train and hurried off to Zebedee's place.

'I've–er–got something to ask you,' Dougal began, with a little cough, as soon as he saw Zebedee.

'Ask away,' said Zebedee, bouncing up and down on his spring. 'Any little problems and I'll do my best to solve them – me and my magic moustache.'

'H'mm – well, yes,' said Dougal. 'It's like this, then. I was asleep last night when something happened . . . I mean, I heard a noise – not the usual kind of night noise you understand, but a noise: the kind that wakes you up. It woke me up; I got out of bed and well, I – er – wandered about . . .'

Zebedee twirled his long black moustache. 'You wandered about, eh! I understand . . . what next?'

'This noise,' went on Dougal, 'it was, to say the least, alarming – and you know me – I'm not easily alarmed. Anyway, at first I thought it was that cheeky young owl having a bit of a hoot by the well – and then I realised it came from the old treacle factory on the hill – you know the one?'

'I do,' said Zebedee. 'It's been empty for years and years. Nobody goes near . . .'

'Exactly,' Dougal said. 'Well, I did. I climbed the hill up to the factory. It was all lit up, which was odd. But more odd – was the voice.'

Dougal broke off at this point and Zebedee said helpfully, 'Do go on, Dougal. What voice . . .?'

'I don't know,' Dougal confessed. 'It was – er – rather a coarse voice – rather common, if you get my meaning. It said something about wanting to serve the Blue Voice . . .'

'You're sure you weren't dreaming?' Zebedee asked.

'Certainly not!' Dougal snapped. 'This other voice; the one that came from inside the factory was quite different – it was really rather feminine, and I can remember what it said:

something about Blue: Blue is beautiful; Blue is best: I am Blue: I am beautiful: I am best . . .'

'Very odd!' said Zebedee, 'Very odd indeed! I never cared for blue.'

'I hate the colour,' said Dougal. 'But you know that old factory looked a ghostly kind of blue last night – and all craggy. I'm quite worried about it.'

Zebedee hesitated. It was quite clear to Dougal that he didn't know what to say. 'I suppose the best thing you can do is to go and talk to Florence about it all,' said Zebedee at last. 'She's such a sensible girl and so sympathetic . . .'

'Sympathetic – what do you mean?' Dougal asked suspiciously. 'You don't think it was just a dream?'

Zebedee didn't answer and with a sad little shake of his head, Dougal walked away.

As Dougal set out for Florence's house, Florence herself was just stepping out into the Magic Garden to talk to Mr. Rusty.

'It's such a lovely day, Mr. Rusty,' said Florence, 'I just couldn't stay inside to do my dusting – so here I am.'

'It's a pleasure to see you,' said old Mr. Rusty. 'Young Paul and Basil were just going to call you. We've got a surprise for you. Such a surprise!'

'What is it?' Florence cried, clapping her hands. 'I do so love surprises – and it's not even my birthday.'

'It's not exactly that kind of a surprise,' said Mr. Rusty, his eyes twinkling. 'Why don't you look behind you, Florence, at the Magic Roundabout . . .'

So Florence turned round and looked at the Magic Roundabout – and there was her surprise! A beautiful blue cat!

'Oh, oh! oh!' exclaimed Florence. 'What a super cat – What a super *blue* cat.'

'Isn't he splendid?' Basil said. 'He's the first blue cat I've ever seen.'

'I'm the only true blue cat you will ever see,' said the blue cat suddenly, and he got up and stretched himself before stepping down from the Magic Roundabout. 'Call me Buxton, will you?'

'That's a pretty name,' said Florence, who had already given her heart to the beautiful blue cat. 'Buxton! I like that!'

Florence was so taken up with the new visitor to the Magic Garden that she forgot all about Dougal.

It was only when Mr. Rusty mentioned that he had just seen a flash of yellow among the trees that Florence thought about him.

'Let's give Dougal a surprise when he comes,' she whispered to Mr. Rusty. 'We'll ask Buxton to hide and then, when I say the word, he can come out from behind that tree . . .'

'Yellow is not my favourite colour,' said Buxton, who had been listening shamelessly to Florence's conversation.

'Oh, you'll just love Dougal,' Florence said quickly. 'And if you wouldn't mind hiding behind that tree . . . oh, quick, he's coming now!'

Obediently, Buxton jumped behind the tree just seconds before Dougal appeared. He carried a bouquet of flowers in his mouth and this he proceeded to lay at Florence's feet. 'For you,' he said, 'just a little trifle I picked up on the way . . .'

'That's very sweet of you, Dougal darling!' cried Florence. 'I have something for you, too, a surprise . . .'

'Not, not – er – a bag of sugar lumps, I suppose?' said Dougal hopefully. 'Or just some sugar cakes?'

'No, nothing like that,' laughed Florence. Then raising her voice, she called, 'Buxton, you can show yourself now. Buxton meet Dougal! Dougal meet Buxton!'

Dougal took several startled steps backwards. 'What – what on earth is it?' he gasped. 'No, no don't tell me . . .' And he bared his teeth.

The news of the blue cat's arrival spread to other parts of the Magic Garden and soon Brian, Dylan and Ermintrude came along to see and admire him.

Dougal tried, in vain, to get Florence's full attention.

'Don't bother me now,' Florence said at last. 'We simply must decide where the blue cat is going to stay.'

Brian gave Dougal one of his sly looks. Then he said, 'What about Dougal's place? He's got a lovely big bed . . .'

'Thanks very much,' said Buxton, who had kept silent whilst this discussion was going on. 'Very nice of you to offer, I'm sure.'

'I didn't offer,' Dougal snapped, and he gave Brian an indignant look. 'I certainly did *not* offer . . .'

But Florence and the others all agreed that Dougal's place was just right for their guest, and Florence said, 'Come along, Buxton. We'll all help you settle in. Dougal's bed is ever so comfy, and I expect you're longing to lie down for a little rest . . .'

As they moved away, Dougal whispered urgently to Florence, 'I really do have a problem, you know. It's about that old treacle factory on the hill . . .'

'Some other time, Dougal darling,' Florence returned. 'Let's get Buxton safely tucked up in bed first.'

With Ermintrude's help, Dougal's bed was quickly made up and, no sooner was Buxton cosily installed, than Florence went off, saying that she was going to bake a lovely fish pie for Buxton's dinner the next day.

For the first time in his life, Dougal found himself left out in the cold.

Feeling thoroughly miserable, he decided at last to pay another visit to the factory on the hill. 'You never know,' he told himself, 'I might find out something more and then maybe they will listen to me . . .'

Alas for Dougal's plan! As he made his way up to the factory gate, he stepped on a mechanical lift; his weight triggered off the mechanism and up shot the lift, taking Dougal with it.

'Help! Help!' Dougal screamed, as he found himself ten feet or more above ground. 'Somebody help me . . .' He choked back his next scream as, suddenly, from his airy platform, he spied a figure coming quickly and stealthily up the hill. It was none other than the blue cat, Buxton.

As Dougal watched, he saw Buxton stop in front of the factory gate and he heard him call out, 'Open up. I've arrived to claim my rights.'

'Who are you?' came a second voice from inside the factory, and Dougal gave such a start that he nearly rolled off his platform. It was the voice he had heard once before; the Blue Voice.

'I'm Buxton, the cat,' answered the blue cat. 'I'm ready to serve the Blue Cause. Ready to wipe out all other colours – especially yellow – down with yellow . . . I'm ready to begin my test.'

'Then enter, blue cat, and prepare to win your crown. Remember there are seven doors that await you,' came the reply.

As the factory gate clanged behind Buxton, the Blue Voice spoke again.

'What is the colour of the first door, Buxton?' it asked, and the blue cat gulped and whispered nervously, 'Blue!'

'Well done, Buxton!' exclaimed the Blue Voice. 'You have passed the first of the tests. You are now a knight!'

Buxton pushed open this first door and found himself in a room where flowers of many colours were all being dyed blue.

'Soon the world will forget what the daisy and the primrose look like!' the Blue Voice cried. 'Soon all the flowers of the world will be blue. Blue is beautiful, Buxton, blue is best. I am blue, I am beautiful, I am best . . . what is the colour of the second door that faces you, Sir Buxton? Answer wrongly and you perish . . .'

'Cobalt blue!' Buxton stammered.

'Right again, Baron Buxton!' exclaimed the Voice. 'Pass on now to my blue room. Down with red and green . . .'

'Down with pink and purple,' muttered Baron Buxton loyally, as he saw bale upon bale of cloth being dyed blue. 'The colour of the third door is Saxony blue!'

'Correct, Lord Buxton,' cried the Voice. 'Pass on now to face the fourth door.'

'It's indigo! Indigo blue,' Lord Buxton screamed, forgetting all his fear.

'Right again, Marquis Buxton,' the Voice told him. 'And now the fifth door . . .'

For a moment Buxton seemed to hesitate. Then he stammered out, 'B-baby b-blue – that's it – Baby blue.'

'Pass now into the room of thunder and lightning, the room of anger and rage, Duke Buxton,' ordered the Voice.

'D-don't tell me!' cried Buxton, his confidence returning. 'I know that colour! It's Prussian blue . . .'

'Well done, Prince Buxton,' answered the Voice. 'This is the room where your soldiers are made. Your soldiers will help you to take over the garden and everything in it. Now tell me – what about the seventh door?'

'It's the door of the Blue King,' Buxton screeched, jumping up and down in his excitement.' I'm King, King, King! I've passed the test. I'm King Buxton the first!'

With a golden crown upon his wicked head and a nasty evil glint in his eye, King Buxton the first took his place upon the royal throne. This was his hour of glory and he meant to enjoy it to the full.

Faced with row upon row of blue soldiers, ready to carry out his slightest command, King Buxton gave a triumphant leer. By pure chance, he had been born blue, the only blue cat in the whole world – the only cat to be considered worthy enough to serve the Blue Cause.

'He's the King, the wickedest, bluest one we've ever had,' chanted the soldiers.

'I'm your King all right,' Buxton shouted. 'And don't you ever forget it. Here is my first command. Everything NOT blue, unless it belongs to me, must be destroyed. Do you understand?'

'We understand!' chanted the soldiers.

'And everyone NOT blue is to be taken prisoner and thrown in the dungeon beneath this fact – er – palace,' Buxton went on, hastily changing the word factory to palace. 'I'm the King. My word is law.'

'You're the King and your word is law!' echoed the soldiers. 'We understand and we obey!'

'That's it, then!' said Buxton, and he straightened his crown.

Meanwhile, back in the Magic Garden, Ermintrude and the others were wondering what had happened to the blue cat.

'Dougal's missing too,' said Brian. 'I wonder if they've both gone off together for a walk?'

'It's hardly likely, darling,' said the little pink cow. 'But I hope dear Buxton comes back soon. I do so want him to see my blue picture. I'm painting it just for him, you know.'

'He can't have gone very far,' Florence said, as Ermintrude took up her paintbrush once again and began daubing sploshes of blue paint on to the canvas. 'You don't suppose anything has happened to him?' Florence went on. 'I just couldn't bear that. You know, I can't quite explain it, but everything that's blue has become ever so important to me, even the flowers. I just love blue flowers now.'

'Don't worry, Florence,' said Brian. 'I tell you what, I'll go and look for him. He might have wandered up the hill and gone down the other side . . .'

'Do that, Brian,' said Florence.

'If I find the blue cat before I find Dougal,' Brian decided as he made his way up the hill towards the factory, 'I'll put in a good word for that obstinate dog . . .'

But as he reached the factory, he heard a voice he knew only too well.

'Help! Help! Let me down – you – you two-horned idiot!'

Two horns Brian might have, but he was certainly no fool! A quick glance upward showed him Dougal suspended, as it were, in mid-air.

'Two-horned idiot, am I?' Brian said to himself, all his kinder feelings about Dougal vanishing in a flash. 'I'll show him.'

And with a sly, mischievous look in his bright eyes, he brought the mechanical lift crashing to the ground, and then skidded away down the hill.

Every bone in Dougal's body was shaken as he hit the ground, but he was so furious with Brian that he scarcely noticed.

'I'll get that Snail one of these days,' he muttered as he picked himself up. 'But first, there are more important things to do. I must warn Florence about the blue cat. She's got to listen. There's something evil going on inside that factory.' And he hurried away down the hill.

But Florence wouldn't listen to Dougal's warning about the blue cat. 'He's a traitor!' Dougal shouted. 'He's up to no good . . .'

'Don't talk such nonsense, Dougal,' was all Florence said. And Ermintrude and Dylan both laughed. 'I guess he's been sitting too long in the sun,' Dylan murmured, and Ermintrude nodded as they left the bridge.

'You really mustn't talk so wildly,' said Florence later, giving Dougal a kindly little pat. 'We all love the blue cat already and we're just anxious to find him, that's all.'

'You'll find him all right!' Dougal said bitterly, 'but it won't turn out as you think. He's probably hatching some fiendish plot to destroy us all this very minute!'

To Florence's surprise, as she turned

away from Dougal, there was the blue cat himself suddenly behind her.

'Dear, dear Buxton!' she cried, 'we thought you were lost . . .'

Buxton sighed and put his head on one side in a most pathetic way which deceived everyone except Dougal.

'I – I couldn't help hearing what Dougal was saying,' he whispered. 'Oh dear, it's always the same wherever I go. Nobody loves me.'

'We love you,' Florence said, giving Dougal a reproachful look. 'We all love you here and we want you to stay with us for ever and for ever . . .' She broke off as Zebedee appeared among them.

He looked so different and so un-happy that they all stared at him. 'Something terrible has happened,' Zebedee said, putting a hand up to his face. 'I've lost my magic moustache. It's been stolen, no doubt of it. And with no moustache, all my magic has gone . . .'

'Don't worry, Zebedee!' Florence cried. 'Your magic moustache must be somewhere in the Magic Garden. We'll all help you to hunt for it. Look, here come Mr. Rusty and Mr. MacHenry. They're awfully good at finding things.'

But Mr. MacHenry and Mr. Rusty had problems of their own. 'We can't understand it,' Mr. MacHenry told Florence. 'There's a rash of blue cactus springing up all over the Magic Garden.'

The Blue Take-over of the Magic Garden was just about to begin!

With a hundred soldiers to command, the blue cat's take-over was soon completed.

Florence and Zebedee were captured, almost at once. So, too, were Mr. Rusty and Mr. MacHenry.

Then came Brian and Ermintrude, who put up a gallant fight.

The blue soldiers dragged them away and thrust them into a dark dungeon under the factory, where they were loaded with chains and left to themselves.

'If only I had my magic moustache,' poor Zebedee whispered to Florence, as she began to cry. 'I could save you all.'

Alas, Zebedee's magic moustache was now in a glass case in Buxton's throne room and Buxton himself was keeping an eye on it.

'So we've got them all!' he gloated, when his soldiers came to report. 'And all these stalagmites and stalactites will keep 'em there for ever. Oh, no doubt about it, I'm a wicked, cunning, far-sighted cat . . . a worthy ruler, if I may say so, of the new Blue Kingdom.'

But King Buxton's glee soon vanished when he presently discovered that Dougal was still free. 'I'll get that yellow dog!' he vowed. 'And when I do, I'll make him squirm. Yes, sir!'

And, in another part of the garden, Dougal was preparing for the greatest adventure of his life.

'It's the only thing to do,' he said to himself, as he jumped into a tub of blue dye. 'If the only way to get inside that factory is by being blue, then I'll be blue.'

As he splashed about in the tub, Dougal thought about Florence. 'She always loved me for myself,' he reflected, as slowly his yellow coat changed colour. 'That villain Buxton altered things a bit, but not for long. I'll rescue all of them, even Brian, then we'll see who is the hero!'

Satisfied, at last, that he was a good true blue, Dougal set off for the factory on the hill. When he reached the gates, he found them locked and barred against him, and for a moment he didn't know what to do.

'Don't give up now, Dougal old boy,' he told himself. 'There's that old mining shaft – now where is it? One step to the left; two steps to the right . . . ah, oh! Help! Help!'

As Dougal shot downwards, he all but lost his fur, but he recovered quickly enough when he found himself in the throne room itself . . . and almost face to face with his old enemy.

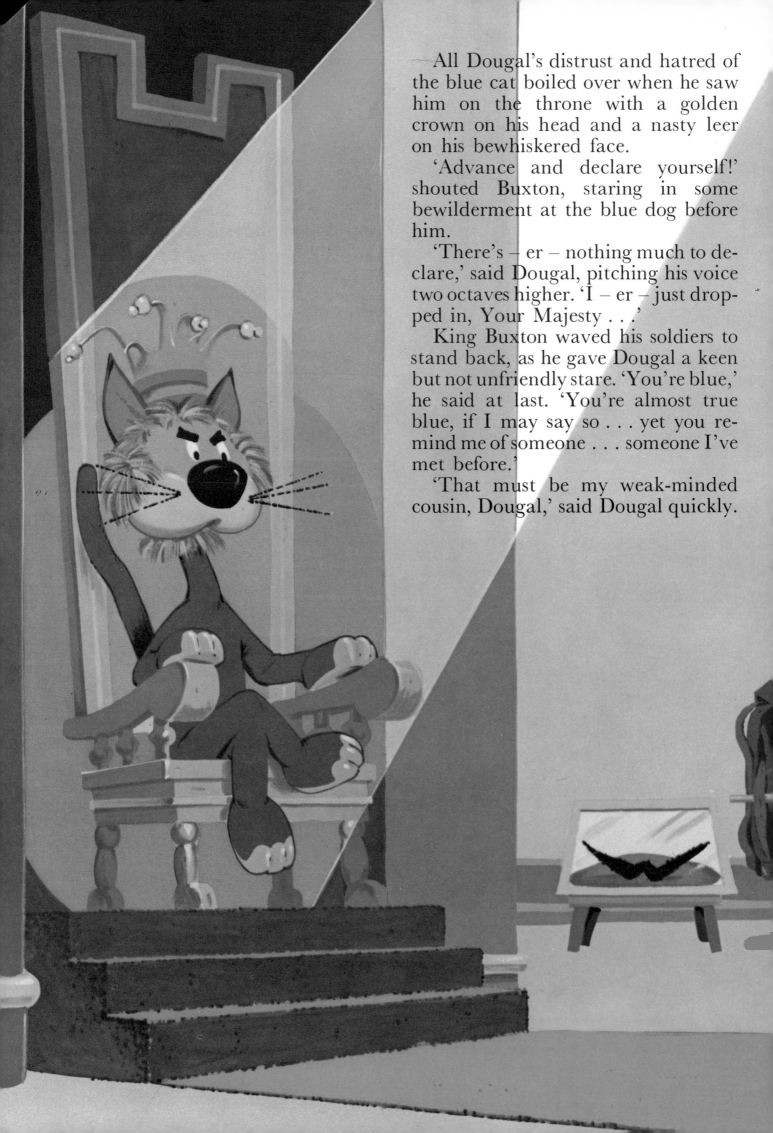

All Dougal's distrust and hatred of the blue cat boiled over when he saw him on the throne with a golden crown on his head and a nasty leer on his bewhiskered face.

'Advance and declare yourself!' shouted Buxton, staring in some bewilderment at the blue dog before him.

'There's – er – nothing much to declare,' said Dougal, pitching his voice two octaves higher. 'I – er – just dropped in, Your Majesty . . .'

King Buxton waved his soldiers to stand back, as he gave Dougal a keen but not unfriendly stare. 'You're blue,' he said at last. 'You're almost true blue, if I may say so . . . yet you remind me of someone . . . someone I've met before.'

'That must be my weak-minded cousin, Dougal,' said Dougal quickly.

'What a han – I mean – miserable fellow he is to be sure. My name's Peter – Blue Peter, in fact . . .'

'What do you want with me?' demanded Buxton, and Dougal told him. 'A cat, sorry, I mean dog, may look at a king, surely? I – er – heard about you; your fame and all that . . .'

'You were right to want to come and admire me,' said Buxton, with a smile. 'I can't blame you for that – but I can't quite place you . . .'

'Don't give it another thought,' said Dougal airily. 'That crazy, sugar-mad cousin of mine with his splen – I mean common yellow coat – must have crossed your path some time or another. You don't want to think about him. I certainly don't. It's quite sickening how he goes on and on about sugar. I can't tell you how I detest the stuff myself . . .'

At the mention of sugar, King Buxton raised himself from his throne. 'Guards!' he shouted. 'Surround him. Take him away to the torture chamber.'

'Hi, wait a minute, you can't do that!' Dougal shouted, in his turn. 'Blue is – er – beautiful . . . blue is b-best.' He got no further for the soldiers took hold of him and dragged him away. As the door of the torture chamber slammed behind Dougal, King Buxton let out a sneering giggle. 'Just let him nibble one small grain of sugar . . . then I'll know who he really is . . .'

As soon as he found himself alone, Dougal looked round his prison; it was packed from floor to ceiling with SUGAR!

Bags of granulated sugar lay all about him – half open – and spilling

over on to the floor. Sugar lumps, the biggest Dougal had ever seen, were stacked up like bricks, and castor sugar flowed, like grains of sand, from an upturned sack . . .'

'Sugar, sugar everywhere and not a grain that's mine!' Dougal moaned. 'Oh, the fiend, the black-hearted villain! What torture to endure! It's too much! Yet – if I as much as crunch one lump of this heavenly sugar – he'll know for certain that I'm the real Dougal and the game's lost . . .'

Dougal licked his lips. The torture was almost too much for him. 'Be a hero,' he told himself. 'Think of

Florence. Think of who you are supposed to be . . . you're Blue Peter; you hate sugar . . .'

'I'm Blue Peter!' he suddenly shouted. 'I hate sugar! Let me out of here! All this heaven – I mean – hateful sugar is making me feel quite sick . . .'

To his great relief, King Buxton himself opened the door.

'Dear friend,' he said. 'You've passed the test. Forgive me, but I had to make absolutely certain that you were not that impudent yellow dog. Welcome to my Blue Kingdom, Prime Minister Blue Peter!'

In his new role as Prime Minister, Dougal was free to make a tour of inspection of the dungeons and his heart nearly broke in two when he saw Florence in chains and heard her singing her sweet, sad song of despair.

But he was given little time to work out a rescue plan.

'The Blue Voice wants us to go to the moon,' Buxton told him. 'The moon must be part of our new blue world, you know.'

'Really,' said Dougal, and then he added, 'Yes, yes, quite right. We must have a blue moon, of course . . .'

As Dougal followed the blue cat

into the space ship, he made up his mind, it would be his last trip ever to the moon.

But, wisely, he kept his mouth firmly shut as the blue cat took over the controls.

'I claim the moon for my Blue Kingdom,' cried Buxton, seconds later, as he climbed down from the rocket on to the moon's surface. And he planted a blue flag which Dougal thought it was just as well to salute. It would be fatal to make a slip at this stage.

'Blue is beautiful. Blue is best,' said Dougal dutifully.

'Well spoken, Prime Minister,' said King Buxton. 'Let us salute the blue flag once more and depart . . .'

'Indeed yes,' said Dougal, taking a step backwards and, horrors, rolling over, straight into a crater.

'Heavens!' he spluttered, as he clambered out. 'There's water on the moon after all. What a discovery!'

But King Buxton, too, was making an amazing discovery. The water had washed off all Dougal's blue dye, and he found himself staring at a yellow dog.

'You're not blue at all!' Buxton screeched. 'You're – you're yellow! You're that yellow dog, Dougal . . .'

'Hey, hold on a minute, Kingy,' Dougal began to protest, but he knew that the game was up. And he backed away from the furious, spitting cat towards the rocket.

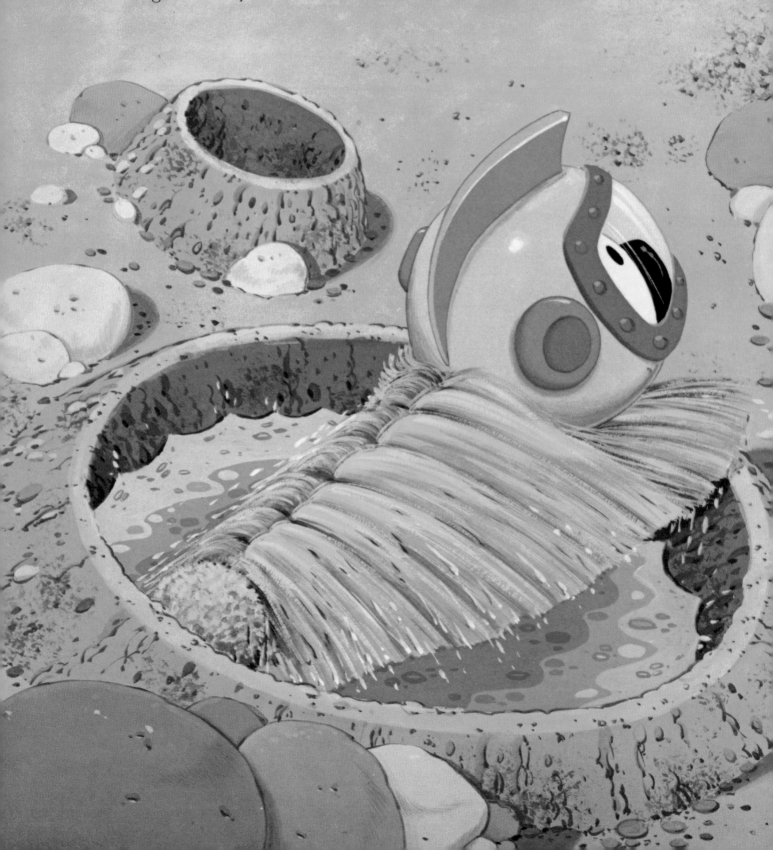

Once inside the rocket, the two fought tooth and claw to gain control and, presently, as it dived earthwards, Dougal took the only possible way out; he left by means of his parachute and floated peacefully downwards.

Buxton, stayed with the rocket until it finally crashed into the factory.

'So you are back already!' said the Blue Voice, from the ruins.

And a miserable Buxton, his conceit all shaken out of him, answered timidly. 'Yes, I am. It all went wrong. That Prime Minister of mine turned out to be that yellow dog, Dougal.'

'He was your choice,' returned the Blue Voice. 'You have failed in your mission. You have lost your chance. There can now be no blue take-over of the Magic Garden. You have failed – failed – failed . . .'

And as the blue cat slunk away, Dougal was already rescuing Florence and all his friends of the Magic Roundabout from the dungeon.

Only Brian was missing when at last they gathered round the Magic Roundabout. And only Zebedee was

sad because he still hadn't found his magic moustache.

But Brian wasn't missing for long. Somewhat to Dougal's annoyance, he soon appeared with Zebedee's magic moustache.

'So now, everything is just as it always was!' cried Zebedee.

'Not quite,' said Dougal. 'We still have to deal with that wicked blue cat . . .'

'Let's forgive him,' said gentle Florence. 'Look, here he is now. See how sad he looks; even his fine whiskers are drooping!'

'I *am* sad,' said the blue cat, coming up to Florence. 'Ever so sad and sorry! Can you forgive me? My heart was in the wrong place, you see. I got carried away. I was too blue.'

'Do forgive him!' Florence cried. 'He must be sorry – or he wouldn't be changing colour. Look everybody! Buxton's ever such a pale blue now!'

'Thank you, one and all,' said Buxton, not meeting Dougal's eye. 'I'd like to stay, if you don't mind. I'll just find myself a little place right at the bottom of the garden. I won't be in anybody's way.'

'You do that!' said Dougal.

Then Mr. Rusty began turning the handle of his barrel organ and, as Florence and her friends joined hands to dance to the music, very very gently, it began to snow.

Perhaps Zebedee had something to do with that. Perhaps he wanted everybody to forget the colour blue. Florence thought so, at any rate, and so did Dougal. But he was much too busy working out how many sugar lumps he was going to eat when the dancing was over, to really care!